STAGE FRIGHT

Bloomsbury Education
An imprint of Bloomsbury Publishing Plc

50 Bedford Square
London
WC1B 3DP
UK

1385 Broadway
New York
NY 10018
USA

www.bloomsbury.com

BLOOMSBURY and the Diana logo are trademarks of Bloomsbury Publishing Plc

First published in 2017 by Bloomsbury Education

A catalogue record for this book is available from the British Library.

ISBN: PB: 978-1-4729-3413-0
         ePub: 978-1-4729-3410-9
         ePDF: 978-1-4729-3412-3

2 4 6 8 10 9 7 5 3 1

Printed in China by Leo Paper Products

This book is produced using paper that is made from wood grown in managed, sustainable
forests. It is natural, renewable and recyclable. The logging and manufacturing processes conform
to the environmental regulations
of the country of origin.

To find out more about our authors and books visit www.bloomsbury.com.
Here you will find extracts, author interviews, details of forthcoming
events and the option to sign up for our newsletters.

recommended by

www.catchup.org

Catch Up is a charity which aims to address the problem of underachievement that
has its roots in literacy and numeracy difficulties.

STAGE FRIGHT

JO COTTERILL

ILLUSTRATED BY
MARIA GARCIA BORREGO

BLOOMSBURY EDUCATION
AN IMPRINT OF BLOOMSBURY
LONDON OXFORD NEW YORK NEW DELHI SYDNEY

CONTENTS

Chapter One

Alice stared out of the car window as her mum drove along the road. They were on their way to Hopewell High, the boarding school where Alice was a pupil. Alice hummed a song as they drove along.

In five weeks the school was putting on the musical 'Legally Blonde' and she was playing the main part of Elle Woods. There were so many lines and songs to remember!

"It's been lovely to hear you singing around the house," Alice's mum said. "You have such a beautiful voice. I don't know where you get it from!"

Alice laughed. "You have a good voice too, Mum. It's just that you never had singing lessons."

"No money for that kind of thing when I was growing up," said her mum. "I just hope you're not getting too worried about the show."

Alice bit her fingernail. "I'm not worried," she said with a laugh. But it was a lie: of · course she was worried. Very worried. Everyone got nervous before a show, didn't they? And she had such a big part!

Her mum gave Alice a quick look. "You will tell me if you have any problems at school, won't you?" she asked.

Alice knew what her mum was talking about. Last year, when Alice was thirteen, she had started to suffer from panic attacks. They were frightening, and at first she thought she was going to die. Panic attacks made you breathe faster and faster, and then you felt like you couldn't breathe any more.

They made the world spin inside your head. If you didn't get control early on, it took hours to recover. Now, Alice always carried a paper bag with her. Breathing into the bag stopped the fast breathing and helped her calm down.

"I haven't had a panic attack for ages," Alice said. She bit her fingernail again.

"That doesn't mean they've gone," her mum said. Then she said, "Alice, I've been meaning to talk about something with you. But there hasn't been the right moment…"

Alice looked across at her mum. "What?"

"Your dad and I…" said her mum. "We… you know we haven't been getting along lately."

Alice felt her stomach sink. "Yes..." She had noticed, of course. Dad had been out a lot. And when he was home, there was a kind of coldness between him and Mum. What was Mum about to say?

"I don't want you to worry," Alice's mum said. She sighed, and pulled over to the side of the road so she could turn to Alice. "Things haven't been right for a while."

"Are you going to split up?" Alice asked quickly.

Her mum looked shocked. "No! Well... no, I hope not."

"You **hope** not?" said Alice, nervously.

"I didn't want to upset you on your way back to school!" Mum said, biting her lip. "It's just that I knew you had noticed. But I'm sure we will sort it out, your dad and me. Maybe I've got it wrong."

Alice frowned. "Maybe you've got **what** wrong?"

"I saw a text message..." her mum began. "It's probably nothing. But... well... it was from another woman."

"Another woman? Who?" asked Alice.

"Someone at work," said her mum.

"What did it say?" asked Alice.

Mum gave a sigh and then said, "I think your dad is having an affair."

Chapter Two

Alice waved her mum goodbye and then she ran up to the Nest, the dormitory she shared with her three best friends. All the dormitories at Hopewell High had names. The Nest was on the top floor and was very cosy.

Daisy, Hani and Samira were all there, unpacking their bags. Alice went in and burst into tears. She told the others what her mum had said about her dad having an affair.

"Oh no!" Daisy put her arms around Alice. "I can't believe it. What a shock."

Alice wiped her eyes. "I was just really surprised, that's all. I didn't see it coming."

"Does your mum know **for sure** that your dad is having an affair?" Daisy asked. Her blue-green eyes were lined with make-up, and her long dark hair hung loose around her shoulders.

"No." said Alice, trying to stop crying. "When she asked him about the text message, he said it was just a joke. And then he wouldn't talk about it any more."

"What did the message say?" asked Hani.

"She wouldn't tell me. But I guess it was... personal. Straight after that, he changed the settings on his phone. New password, new lock screen. Now Mum doesn't know who's texting him and can't find out."

"It might be a one-off," said Samira.

"Also," Alice went on, "last week, he went out with his mates. Or at least, he **said** that's where he was going. But Mum bumped into one of his mates the next day and he didn't know anything about it!"

Everyone was silent for a moment.

"That doesn't sound good," Daisy said at last.

"Yeah," said Hani. "No wonder your mum is freaking out. What's she going to do?"

"I don't know. I'm so worried. I wish I didn't have to come back to school." Alice's eyes filled with tears again.

"Group hug!" said Daisy, and she, Samira and Hani put their arms around Alice. "Don't worry," said Daisy. "We are here. You can talk to us any time."

"And I've got to do 'Legally Blonde'!" cried Alice. Her breathing was getting faster.

"Bag!" shouted Daisy.

Samira grabbed a paper bag from the drawer of Alice's bedside table. She handed it to Alice, whose breaths were starting to make a funny hooting sound.

"Breathe into the bag," said Daisy in a firm voice.

Alice's fingers were shaking. She opened the bag and held it over her mouth and nose. The bag filled with air as Alice breathed out and then the bag emptied as she breathed in. Slowly, she calmed down.

The others waited until Alice was ready to take the bag away from her mouth. Then Samira said, "Now lie down and rest."

Alice's eyes were closing. She felt so tired! She heard Daisy say, "I'll go and tell Miss Redmond she's had a panic attack."

"Don't tell her why," said Alice sleepily.

"Don't worry," said Daisy. "We won't tell anyone about your dad. Go to sleep now."

Alice lay down on her bed and fell fast asleep.

Chapter Three

The next day, Alice was in the rehearsal for 'Legally Blonde'.

"Alice!" called out Miss Anya. "You missed your cue again!"

Alice jumped. "I'm so sorry, Miss Anya."

The drama teacher turned to the girl playing the piano. "Take it from the top again, Robin."

Alice stood in the middle of the stage and began to sing her song. Miss Anya watched her carefully.

At the end of the rehearsal, Miss Anya spoke to Alice. "What's going on? You're missing cues, forgetting lines. Didn't you practise over half term?"

Alice felt tears fill her eyes. She had done nothing **but** practise! But since her mum had told her about her dad, Alice had found it impossible to concentrate. Even on acting – her favourite thing!

Miss Anya said gently, "Alice, you have a real gift for acting and singing. But you just don't seem to have your heart in it at the moment. I need you to do your best."

"Sorry, Miss Anya," said Alice miserably. "I'll do better. I just had a hard day."

Miss Anya nodded. "Make sure you get a good night's sleep. The show is only four weeks away, and we've got a lot to get through."

Alice grabbed her script and turned to leave the hall. Robin gave her a friendly smile as she walked past the piano. All the girls knew something was wrong. Alice was usually amazing on stage. It was like a different girl had taken her place.

Alice went straight to the toilets and locked herself in a cubicle. She sat down on the closed seat, breathing heavily. It had been a week since she got back to school, and things at home seemed to be getting worse. Every evening she spoke to her mum on the phone – and every evening her mum got upset. "What will I do if he is having an affair?" she cried. Alice didn't know how to answer.

Alice closed her eyes. Everything was just too much right now. She needed to focus on the musical. If she didn't pull her socks up, Miss Anya might not let her play Elle in the show. And Alice loved the part!

Alice's breathing got faster and faster. By the time she realised, it was too late – the panic attack was in full flow. There was a paper bag in her school bag, but Alice's hands were shaking so much she couldn't grip anything. Her brain shut down, and she began to make little hooting noises with each breath. She slid sideways, until she was crouched in a ball on the floor.

All she could feel was the air going in and out of her lungs – too little, too quickly – and the pounding pressure in her head. Everything else was black.

Chapter Four

"Alice, can you hear me?"

Alice slowly opened her eyes to see Samira looking down at her. "You need to get up now." Alice sat up, feeling very groggy. She was in her own bed, and sunlight was pouring in through the windows. "What time is it?" she asked.

"Half seven," Samira told her. "You will miss breakfast if you don't get a move on. The others have already gone down."

"Half seven... in the morning?" asked Alice.

Samira smiled. "Yeah. You slept through both bells. In fact you've been asleep for about twelve hours."

Alice tried to remember what had happened. "I passed out..." she said.

"You had another panic attack." Samira nodded. "A really bad one. I found you on the floor of the toilets. They had to break the lock on the door to get to you. I've never seen you like that before. Did you forget to take a bag with you or something?"

Alice lay back against her pillows and stared at the ceiling. "No," she said. "I had a bag with me. I just didn't think to get to it until it was too late."

"You know..." Samira began, and then stopped. "If you had fallen against the toilet and hit your head... Alice, I was really worried about you."

"Oh, Sammy, it's OK." Alice sat up to give her friend a hug. "I'm all right, really. And I need to get up! I can't believe I slept so long! I really need a wee!"

Samira smiled as Alice rushed to the bathroom. Then she went downstairs to join Daisy and Hani at breakfast. "She seems OK," she told them. "But she's so stressed. Doing 'Legally Blonde' and worrying about her parents..."

"She's going to have more and more attacks at this rate," said Daisy, taking a bite of toast. "We've got to do something."

"She mustn't miss the show," said Hani. "She's so amazing. If we could stop her worrying about her parents, that would help."

"But we can't do anything about her parents," said Samira. "I mean, what do **we** know about marriage problems?"

"My parents split up when I was eight," said Daisy. "But I never knew half of what was going on."

"It's none of our business if her dad is having an affair," said Samira firmly.

Daisy put down her toast. "What if he **isn't**?" Samira and Hani stared at her. "No, listen," Daisy went on. "What if Alice's mum has got it wrong? I mean, she might be dead right – but what if she isn't? What if something else is going on?"

"Like what?" asked Hani.

But before Daisy could answer, Alice came into the dining room. Daisy quickly started talking about homework, and the others joined in.

For the rest of that day, Daisy's brain was spinning. How could they find out what was really going on at Alice's home?

Chapter Five

It was a week later and Alice was at another rehearsal for 'Legally Blonde'. They were going through all the scenes in the first half of the show but Alice couldn't concentrate.

Only half an hour ago, she had phoned home to see how her mum was.

"He's out again," her mum had said, sounding upset. "He's out at the same time every week, and he won't tell me where. I've tried all his friends, but none of them are with him. I think he must be with **her**."

"But who **is** she?" asked Alice.

Her mum didn't know. "Someone from work," she kept saying. "They have got a new receptionist. Whenever I mention her, he blows his top. Says I'm imagining things. I'm almost sure it's her."

"Oh, Mum..." said Alice.

And now Alice was on the stage, trying to listen to her teacher.

"If you make a mistake," Miss Anya said to the girls, "just find a way to keep going. It's more important that we get through it all. We will work out what went wrong afterwards."

Alice nodded. Everyone went to the sides of the stage, ready to begin.

Alice tried to focus. But in her very first scene, her mind went blank. There was an awful silence. She could hear whispers from behind her: "She's forgotten her line."

"Tell her what it is," said someone.

"No," said another girl, "Miss Anya said we had to get through without a prompt."

Alice looked around the hall in panic. On stage, the other actors looked at her. What was the line? She knew it! But the harder she tried to remember, the further away it seemed.

She felt her breathing getting faster and her hands begin to shake.

Alice knew what was coming. She had to get off the stage, right now. She had to get out!

She started to run down the steps from the stage. But there were props for the play on the steps, and she caught her foot, and tripped...

There was a loud gasp from the rest of the actors as Alice fell hard onto the floor of the hall. People rushed to help, but she had already curled up into a ball with her eyes tight shut.

"Alice?" It was Miss Anya's voice. The hall was empty; everyone else had gone. Alice sat with her back against the front of the stage, a paper bag in her hand. She was exhausted. Miss Redmond was there too. "Alice," Miss Anya was saying, "we can't go on like this."

"Perhaps you should see the school counsellor again," said Miss Redmond. "What do you think?"

Alice nodded. "All right," she said. She had seen Mrs Whittle last year for help with the panic attacks. The counsellor was nice, and she didn't make Alice feel like an idiot.

Then Miss Anya spoke again. "Alice," she said, "we need to talk about the show. There are only three weeks to go, and I'm worried about you."

"I don't think now is the right time," Miss Redmond said.

"I understand that Alice is very tired," Miss Anya said in a gentle voice, "but this is important. If Alice is not able to play the part of Elle, I need as much time as possible to rehearse a different student."

Alice felt her heart sink. "I can do it," she said. She rubbed her elbow, which she had bumped when she fell. "I don't know how, but I'll... I'll fix it. Please, Miss Anya. Please don't take the part away. I love it so much."

Miss Anya sighed. "All right. You've got one week to turn this around. And then I won't have any choice. I can't let all the other students down. They've worked so hard." She smiled. "You're a fantastic performer, Alice, but you won't make it as an actor if you can't control your stage fright. Get on top of this, and you will be a star."

Chapter Six

"Right, here's the plan," said Daisy. She, Hani and Samira were all in the Nest while Alice was at a play rehearsal. It was only three days since Alice's attack in the hall, but Daisy had decided that they had to do something.

"We know that Alice's dad got a text message from another woman," Daisy said. "Right?"

"Right," agreed Hani.

"And that Alice's mum saw it, and thought it was suspicious," went on Daisy. "So it must have been a flirty message, right?"

"Right," agreed Samira.

"But," said Daisy, "we don't know what it said. Or what he wrote back. The text message is Clue One."

Hani looked at Samira. "She thinks we are in a detective story."

"Clue Two," said Daisy. "Where is Alice's dad going at the same time each week? Who is he meeting, and why?"

"They live a hundred miles away," Samira said. "We can't exactly follow him to see."

"And Clue Three," went on Daisy. "The new receptionist where he works. The one he goes funny about when she's mentioned." She sat back, satisfied. "Well?"

Hani shook her head. "I don't see how we can find out anything," she said.

Daisy rolled her eyes. "You've got no imagination."

"Running is my thing," Hani said. "Not thinking."

"Alice's dad works for a company that makes computer software," said Daisy. "And every company has a website. Look…" She opened her laptop and showed them what she'd found.

"That's Alice's dad!" said Samira. There on the screen was a photograph of him in a business suit. His name, job title and email address were underneath. "You're not going to **email** him?!"

"Nope." Daisy pointed to a list of names on the side of the page. "I'm more interested in **this**."

Samira leaned forward to see. "It's everyone who works for the company... including the receptionists."

Daisy pointed at a name. "Anna Moss," she said. "She only joined the company two months ago. And now..." She swung the laptop round and typed quickly. Then she turned it back to the other two. "There she is."

On the screen was a photo of a woman in her twenties. She was smiling at the camera. She wore a pink top and a thin silver necklace, and she was very pretty.

"How did you...?" asked Hani.

"The internet," said Samira simply. "You can find anyone, anywhere, these days..."

Daisy nodded. "Yup. So now we know her name and what she looks like. And she's **gorgeous**, which doesn't look good."

"But we still don't know..." began Hani.

"But we can try and find out," said Daisy. "You two can find out where she went to school, her previous job, newspaper items, all sorts."

Samira and Hani looked at each other. "Isn't that illegal?" Samira asked.

"It's **research**," said Daisy firmly. "And I'm going to tackle Clue Two: where he goes each week at the same time."

"He's meeting someone," said Hani.

Daisy nodded. "And how does everyone arrange meetings these days? Email." She clicked 'page back' on her laptop. "There's his email address. And it just so happens that I'm going out with the biggest tech-head in the country. I'm going to ask Storm to hack into Alice's dad's email."

Chapter Seven

Alice came out of her visit to the counsellor feeling better. Mrs Whittle had been very kind. "Don't blame yourself for having panic attacks," she advised. "It's not something to be ashamed of. And we will get on top of it, I promise.

I have spoken to your mum as we agreed, and she knows you're worried about things at home. Your mum says she won't phone you as often if it makes things worse. It sounds like your mum and dad are going through a rough patch – lots of marriages do – and I'm sure things will settle down again soon."

She had given Alice a few new things to try, to keep herself calm. So Alice was feeling a lot more confident when she went back to her rehearsal, and Miss Anya was delighted at the difference. "Well done, Alice!" she said at the end. "That's more like it!"

The other girls in the cast were pleased too – so, when Alice set off for dinner, she was feeling a lot happier.

Her friends were all talking at the dinner table, but as soon as they saw her, they stopped. "Hi!" said Daisy, with a fake smile. "How did rehearsal go?"

"OK..." said Alice. "What were you guys talking about?"

"Er..." Hani looked at the other two, her eyes wide. "Er... the 1500 metres race next Saturday. I've been training hard but I was telling Daisy and Sammy that I didn't feel confident I would win."

"Yes!" Sammy added quickly. "And I said that, of course, she would win. She's easily our best 1500 metre runner."

They all smiled at her. Alice was quite sure it was a total lie but why would her best friends lie to her? Unless... unless they had been talking about **her**?

All of a sudden, Alice found she didn't want any dinner.

* * *

Much, much later that night, everyone in the Nest was asleep. Everyone, that is, except for Daisy, who was hiding under her duvet with her smartphone.

Daisy was addicted to her smartphone – and also to her boyfriend, Storm. The two of them messaged each other every night. Storm went to an all-boys school that was also a technology college. He was ace at programming and coding.

Daisy had asked Storm to hack into Alice's dad's email account. Now, she typed quickly...

Cutie: what did you find out? Did you get in OK?

Thunder: you are insane. I can't just hack into someone's personal emails. Do you know the trouble I would be in if I got caught?

Cutie: what?? I thought everyone hacked these days. Isn't it easy?

Thunder: It might be easy but it's also illegal. You will have to find another way. Sorry, Daisy.

Cutie: oh. Oh OK.

Thunder: don't be like that! Look, I'll send you a stupid pic instead.

Storm's photo was of him pulling a silly face. Normally, Daisy would have laughed, but she didn't feel at all amused. How on earth would they find out what was going on now?

Chapter Eight

It was two days later and Hani, Daisy and Samira were finishing their evening meal.

Alice had gone off to her final dress rehearsal, having eaten almost none of her food.

She should have been excited, but instead she just looked pale and sad.

"I guess there's nothing else we can do," Hani said. Samira nodded. Daisy hated that they hadn't been able to solve the problem. She didn't like anyone or anything to get the better of her, but she had to admit she had run out of ideas. The three girls cleared their plates and set off for their dormitory.

"I'm going to check the post," Samira said. "Hang on a sec." She dashed off down the corridor for a moment and came back holding two letters. "I think this letter might be more info on my course in the holidays – the science one. I'm really looking forward to it!

Oh, and this one was in your pigeon-hole."
She handed over an envelope to Daisy.

"Thanks." Daisy hardly looked at it. She was still trying to work out how to help Alice. Maybe she could catch a train to Alice's home town and ask around there? But who would tell her? She couldn't just turn up at Alice's house and demand to know what was going on... or could she?

Samira and Hani chatted all the way up the stairs, but Daisy didn't hear a word. When they arrived at the Nest, she sat down on her bed. There must be **something**...

She didn't even look at the envelope as she slid her finger along the fold to open the letter Samira had given her. There was one sheet of paper inside, handwritten. Daisy frowned. Who would write an old-fashioned letter these days, when email was so much quicker?

She started reading... and her eyes opened wider and wider. And then she checked the name on the envelope.

The letter wasn't for her at all – it was for Alice.

And it explained **everything**!

Daisy leaped off her bed and ran down the stairs, nearly knocking over some younger girls on the way. She had to tell Alice. Right now!

But the doors to the school hall were all closed, and, from behind them, Daisy could hear singing. The dress rehearsal had already started. And there was no way of telling Alice about the letter for another two hours!

Chapter Nine

Alice got through the rehearsal on automatic. The notes were pitch-perfect and her lines were correct, but her heart wasn't in it.

In the final number, Alice saw Daisy creep into the back of the hall. Alice bit her lip.

Her friends had been acting so oddly recently. They were always whispering, and when they saw her, they stopped. Maybe her panic attacks were too much for them. Had Daisy come to tell Alice they didn't want her in the Nest any more?

Miss Anya praised everyone for their performances. When she got to Alice, she gave her a warm smile and squeezed her shoulder. But Alice knew her drama teacher was disappointed. She could do better – everyone knew that. With a heavy heart, she got changed and went out into the hall.

"We need to talk," said Daisy. Her voice was urgent. "Not here – back in the Nest.

There's something we have to tell you."

Alice nodded. Here it was, then – the bad news. She followed Daisy up the stairs without speaking. Hani and Samira were waiting for them. Daisy shut the door.

"I just want to say," Daisy started, "that this was a **total** accident."

"It was my fault really," added Samira. "The letter was in the wrong pigeon-hole. I thought it was for Daisy."

Alice was confused. "What letter?"

Daisy held out a torn envelope. "This one. It's for you. It's from your dad. I'm so sorry – I read it before I realised it was for you."

Alice stared at the envelope, at her dad's neat handwriting. Her knees felt wobbly and she sank down onto a bed. Was he writing to say that they were getting a divorce? "I don't want to read it."

Samira sat down next to her. "You must," she said gently. "Don't be scared. It's not what you think."

"It's not what any of us thought!" Hani added.

"Your dad isn't having an affair," burst out Daisy.

Alice's mouth fell open. "What? What are you talking about?"

"Every week when he goes out," said Daisy, "he's not meeting a woman. He's seeing a counsellor. Your dad is in therapy for depression."

Chapter Ten

Alice read the letter:

Dear Alice,

I'm so sorry to hear you've been having panic attacks again. I feel really bad that I may have caused them. I know your mum is very sad and confused right now, and I'm trying to put things right.

I've been suffering from stress for a while. I think I've made it worse by trying to hide it – like when you try to fight a panic attack, it just gets worse. I don't enjoy my job very much, and I'm so very tired all the time. I want to shake off this depression so I've been going to see a counsellor every week. He's helping me sort out my head.

I haven't told your mum because I don't want to worry her. But now she's got hold of the wrong end of the stick, and somehow whatever I say is wrong. I've been putting off telling her, but I will, I promise. I'll sort it all out, don't worry.

I'm looking forward to coming to see you in the show! See you soon, sweetheart.

Dad xx

Alice felt a great weight lift from her shoulders. Dad was in therapy! Not having an affair! They weren't getting divorced! But that still left... "What about the receptionist and the text message?" she asked.

Samira nodded. "It's no wonder your mum got suspicious. The receptionist is called Anna Moss, and she's all over social media. She's really flirty – leaves comments that... well..." Samira blushed. "They're kind of rude, you know? She's always getting into trouble for flirting with other people's boyfriends. So I think she's probably trying to flirt with your dad, and he doesn't want to know. He can't exactly avoid her because she works in his building."

"Plus," added Hani, "if he's depressed and struggling, that won't help."

"He's probably hoping that Anna Moss will just leave him alone," said Samira.

Alice didn't know whether to laugh or cry. "He's such a... oh, Dad! You idiot, why didn't you just tell Mum right from the start?"

"It's a man thing," Daisy said. "My dad is just the same. But now **you** can tell her." She picked up Alice's phone and handed it to her, smiling. "Get your parents talking to each other."

Chapter Eleven

Alice peeped through the gap in the stage curtain. The audience was still coming in, and her eyes searched the hall. Where were they? Mum had promised they would be here!

"Alice!" Miss Anya tried to pull her away. "Someone will see you. Go to the side of the stage."

"Please, Miss Anya," Alice said, holding tightly to the curtain. "I need to see my parents."

Miss Anya shook her head but she was smiling.

And just then, Alice saw them. Her mum – **and** her dad – making their way towards the front of the audience to their reserved seats. Her mum was turning to say something to her dad, and they were smiling at each other. Alice felt almost sick with relief. It was all right! They were all right!

It hadn't been an easy conversation when Alice had phoned home two days before. At first, her mum had refused to believe it.

"Why wouldn't he tell me he was seeing a counsellor?"

"It's a man thing," Alice said. "Daisy said her dad is the same."

"And he wrote it to you in a letter?" Her mum sounded amazed. "He hasn't used pen and paper for **years**."

"Mum," Alice said. "Go and talk to him. Right now."

A little later, her mum had rung back. And then her dad had come to the phone too, and it had been a bit awkward, but then it was nice.

He wasn't cross that she'd told her mum.

Maybe that's what he was hoping for when he wrote the letter.

Alice had not had any more panic attacks. She knew that she might have attacks some time in the future, but not right now. She no longer felt like the world was falling apart.

"Alice!" whispered Miss Anya. "You must come away from the curtain now – we are about to start!"

Alice took one last look at her parents, who were sitting holding hands, and she smiled to herself.

The music started up. And then the curtains opened, and the show started – and Alice stepped out onto the stage and sang her heart out.

Bonus Bits!

QUIZ TIME

See how good your knowledge of the story is by answering these multiple-choice questions. Look back at the story for help if you need to.

1. What part is Alice playing in the school play?
   a Ellie Woods
   b Elle Woods
   c Elsa Woods

2. What had Alice started to suffer from when she was 13?
   a Asthma
   b Hayfever
   c Panic attacks

3. Why did Alice's mum think Alice's dad was having an affair in the first place?

  a She saw a text message from another woman on his phone.

  b He lied about where he was going.

  c He told her he didn't love her.

4. Which floor is the Nest on?

  a Ground

  b Second

  c Top

5. Why did Alice trip on the stage steps?

  a Her leg gave way.

  b She jumped too many steps.

  c There were props on the steps.

WHERE TO GET HELP

Alice is taking part in a big performance. This is something she loves but it brings stress and anxiety. She would usually be able to cope with this but she is worried about her parents arguing.

If you have concerns and worries about things, and don't feel able to talk to your friends or family, there are people who can help.

Childline

Childline is a free, 24-hour counselling service for everyone under 18. Childline says, "You can talk to us about anything. No problem is too big or too small. We're on the phone and online. However you choose to contact us, you're in control. It's free, confidential and you don't have to give your name if you don't want to."

www.childline.org.uk / telephone: 0800 1111

Mind

Mind is a charity for people with mental health problems. It can provide help and information if you or someone you know is suffering from panic attacks like Alice. It is for adults and children.

www.mind.org.uk / telephone: 0300 123 3393 / text: 86463

ANSWERS to QUIZ TIME
1b 2c 3a 4c 5c